W9-CRF-583

Dorothy and the
Seven-Leaf Clover

DATE DUE

Dorothy and the Seven-Leaf Clover

By Dorothy Haas
Illustrated by David Rose

Random House New York

To Joan and Lee and happy Thanksgivings.
—D.H.

Text copyright © 1985 by Random House, Inc. Illustrations copyright © 1985 by David S. Rose. All rights reserved under International and Pan-American Copyright Conventions. Published in the United States by Random House, Inc., New York, and simultaneously in Canada by Random House of Canada Limited, Toronto.

Library of Congress Cataloging in Publication Data: Haas, Dorothy F. Dorothy and the seven-leaf clover. SUMMARY: When Toto disappears while they are visiting their friends in Oz, Dorothy finds him caught by an unusual Golden Boy who is under the spell of the Wicked Witch of the West. 1. Children's stories, American. [1. Fantasy] I. Rose, David S., 1947–   ill. II. Title. PZ7.H1124Do   1985   [Fic]   84-16080 ISBN: 0-394-87037-9 (trade); 0-394-97037-3 (lib. bdg.)

Manufactured in the United States of America   1 2 3 4 5 6 7 8 9 0

Contents

"Come Back, Toto!"

Dorothy was curled up in the shade of an apple tree, talking to her little dog, Toto.

"Oh, Toto," she said, "when I'm here in Kansas, I miss my friends in the Land of Oz—especially the Scarecrow and the Tin Woodman and the Cowardly Lion, who isn't really the least bit cowardly. But when I'm in Oz, I miss Aunt Em and Uncle Henry."

Toto barked, almost as though he understood what Dorothy was saying. With a flick of his

7

tongue, he reached up and kissed her chin.

Dorothy laughed. She bit off a piece of the apple she was eating and offered it to him on the palm of her hand.

He sniffed at it and she fondled his silky ears. "But you are always with me, darling Toto, whether I'm here or there."

She pulled a handkerchief from her pocket. "It's Saturday morning, Toto. Do you know what that means? I can wave my hanky and the Princess Ozma will see me in her magic picture and whisk me back to Oz."

Holding Toto tightly, she flicked the handkerchief.

There was a whistle of wind and a whirl of light, and before Dorothy blinked, she was set down in the shade of another tree. Almost at once there was a popping noise like the sound of bubbles bursting, and the Scarecrow and the Tin Woodman and the Cowardly Lion were standing around her, all talking at once.

" . . . thousand and three gold coins," the Scarecrow was saying.

" . . . a day of rejoicing every second Tuesday," the Tin Woodman was saying.

" . . . decree of the day is to be . . . " the Cowardly Lion was saying.

They looked bewildered. Then—

"Little Dorothy!" said the Tin Woodman.

"Little Dorothy Gale!" said the Scarecrow.

"Little Dorothy Gale from Kansas!" said the Lion.

Dorothy leaped to her feet, spilling Toto into the grass. She hugged all of them. And they hugged her back. The Tin Woodman was especially careful not to clasp her too tightly in his strong metal arms.

"I was in the midst of giving a royal order of rejoicing to the Winkies," said the Tin Woodman. "Now they can just keep on rejoicing until I return."

"I was counting the gold coins in the royal treasury," said the Scarecrow. "I'm sure my third helper will keep on counting until I get back."

"It was almost breakfast time in the forest," said the Lion. "I'm sure my subjects will be happy

to play all day before hearing the rest of the royal decree. I love my forest kingdom," he added, "but I'm happiest when we are all together."

"Oh, I've missed you all so much," said Dorothy. Then, as Toto darted off after a squirrel, she called, "Toto, come back."

Toto looked back at Dorothy. Then he watched the squirrel for a moment. The squirrel scampered up a tree and sat on a low branch, scolding.

Toto turned and came back to Dorothy.

Dorothy scooped him up. "It's a while since we've been here in Oz," she said, tapping his nose with her finger. Toto licked the finger. "You must remember that things here aren't what they seem to be. You must stay near me."

She set him down. "Now, walk beside me," she warned him.

And Toto did.

He didn't run after a rabbit that poked its head up out of the grass.

He ignored a chipmunk that darted out of their path.

But then a field mouse ran past under his very

nose. And Toto could not resist field mice. With a yip he dashed after the small creature.

The field mouse ran toward a nearby cornfield. So did Toto.

The field mouse disappeared among the standing corn—and Toto did too. He didn't hear Dorothy calling him.

"Come back, Toto!" she shouted. "Come back. You can get lost among tall cornstalks."

She ran toward the cornfield, followed by the Scarecrow and the Tin Woodman and the Lion. They bumped into one another when she stopped suddenly at the edge of the field.

"I've never seen funny-looking corn like this," she said.

"Can't say as I've paid much attention to corn," said the Lion.

"But I have," said the Scarecrow, "and Dorothy is right. Corn is supposed to stand straight and tall."

"But these cornstalks are all twisted and curled," said Dorothy.

In the distance Toto's barking grew fainter.

Dorothy took a few steps forward. "Someone can be lost in a cornfield almost forever," she said, "or at least until harvest time. But I can't let Toto be lost!" And she plunged in among the tangled stalks. The Scarecrow and the Tin Woodman and the Lion followed her.

And then, how strangely things happened. The queer, twisted stalks seemed to bend away in front of the four friends, making a path into the field.

"Very courteous cornstalks, I must say," said the

Scarecrow. "I wonder who taught them their manners."

The faster the friends ran, the more swiftly the cornstalks parted, opening a way deeper and deeper into the field.

Dorothy stopped, quite out of breath.

"I don't know much about cornfields," said the Tin Woodman, "but this one seems to be acting odd."

"If I weren't so brave a creature," said the Lion, "I might almost be afraid. Which, of course, I am not."

"It does seem to me," said the Scarecrow, "that cornstalks should not weave together behind us as these seem to be doing."

Dorothy looked back the way they had come. The cornstalks had indeed woven into a solid wall behind them. And the way on both sides of them was braided together as well.

"Oh, my," whispered Dorothy. "Oh, my."

And now she couldn't hear Toto's bark at all.

The Enchanted Cornfield

As Dorothy stood looking around, wondering, fearful for Toto, a rustling whisper arose from the cornstalks. *Ohhhhhhhh.* The sound hung in the air.

The friends crowded more closely together.

Dorothy bit her lip, trying to understand the sound. Was it angry? Sad? One that meant trouble for all of them?

And the murmur continued. *Ahhhhhhhhhh.*

Hands on her hips, Dorothy turned from side

to side, looking, looking. "Now, you just see here," she said firmly, not sure whom she was speaking to. "I don't know why you're making that noise—"

Ohhhhhhhhhh. The sound curled around them.

"—or why you're all tangled up," Dorothy went on, "but you just stop it right now. You can't keep us prisoners here."

The soft moaning didn't stop. The cornstalks didn't untwist themselves from their woven wall. The only ones that moved opened a way farther into the cornfield. They bent and bowed and swayed as though inviting her to move ahead.

But was it safe to go forward?

Dorothy stood, uncertain. What was she to do? Toto was somewhere in this field, and maybe the strange cornstalks were keeping him prisoner. She no longer heard his voice. "Oh, Toto," she whispered.

"Something must be done," said the Lion. "Stand back. This is not for the faint of heart."

He threw back his great head and roared. The deep sound lifted around them and rolled over the cornfield like thunder. "Move back, I command you!" he roared. "I am King of the Beasts."

The cornstalks didn't stir. Not the woven wall that blocked their way out of the field, nor the

braided cornstalks on either side of them. And still the whispering sigh floated in the air.

"Thunderation," said the Lion. "I am not used to refusals to obey."

He sat down, quite bewildered.

The Tin Woodman stepped forward. "Let the chips fall where they may," he said. He lifted his axe and gave a mighty swing at the thickest cornstalk.

The axe rang against the stalk and bounced back. The Tin Woodman staggered. And the cornstalk was not even scratched.

"An enchantment," he whispered. "This cornfield is under a spell."

"Toto is somewhere in the middle of it," said Dorothy. Her voice quavered. "What can have happened to him?"

The Scarecrow had been standing to one side, his hand covering his eyes, in deepest thought. Now he spoke. "It is my opinion," he said, "that we should go that way." He pointed to the path that lay open among the cornstalks. "As it is the only way to go," he added.

"You are so sensible, old friend," said Dorothy.

"What would I do without you!" Then, fearful that she might hurt the feelings of the Tin Woodman and the Lion, she quickly added, "Or any of you."

Dorothy led the way, running, moving ever deeper into the cornstalk jungle. From time to time she paused, listening, listening. "Toto!" she called. "Toto, can you hear me?" But there was no answering bark.

They ran for what seemed like hours over the bumpy earth. After a time the cornstalks thinned out and there was more space between them.

"Maybe we're coming to something," panted Dorothy, stopping to listen. "Toto?" she called again.

A faint bark answered her.

"We're close to him!" said Dorothy. She lifted her voice. "We're coming, Toto!" she called.

As they ran, the little dog's barking grew louder. And at last they stumbled into a clearing. No cornstalks grew here. Only a few pumpkins lay scattered in the open space. Standing in the very center was an old-fashioned summerhouse, a place to rest from the heat of the sun.

The walls of the summerhouse were made of braided cornstalks that permitted the breezes to pass through. Its roof was made of corn still within the shucks. All of it, walls and roof, glittered in the sunlight.

"That doesn't look like your ordinary everyday corn," said the Scarecrow, "and I myself, ahem, am an expert on the subject."

Dorothy stepped close. "It's made of gold," she said with wonder. "It's a golden summerhouse."

And Toto was inside.

Dorothy could see him in the cool shadows, leaping against the golden mesh of the walls, trying to reach her. He was yipping with happiness.

She knelt down on the rough earth. "Toto, didn't I tell you to be careful?" she said softly. "And didn't I tell you that things here in Oz are not always what they seem to be?"

She reached toward one of the openings in the golden network to touch his head.

The opening snapped shut.

She snatched her hand away just in time.

3

The Golden Summerhouse

Dorothy sat back on her heels, rubbing her hand, glad she still had all of her fingers. Toto could touch the walls inside the summerhouse. But nobody could touch the outside. "Toto," she whispered comfortingly, "I'll get you out of there. Don't you fret."

But how? How?

Toto whimpered and trotted back and forth on the other side of the wall.

The Tin Woodman walked around the golden

summerhouse. "There is no door," he announced, coming back to where Dorothy knelt. "There are no windows, either."

Dorothy leaned close to the glittering wall, trying to see into the shadows inside. The openings between the golden cornstalks had begun to widen once more.

"Be careful, friend," said the Lion, "or you'll get your nose pinched off."

"Now, that's something I don't have to worry about," said the Scarecrow. "Mine is painted on my face, you know." He crouched beside Dorothy and peered into the strange little house. And so he saw what she saw.

Inside, sitting on a golden bench, was a handsome golden boy. He gave off a golden glow in the shadows.

"Oh, my!" gasped Dorothy. "You're beautiful!"

"I know," said the Golden Boy. His voice was harsh and hollow sounding. But he smiled and bowed his head regally, as a king might.

"But whatever are you doing in there?" asked Dorothy. "And"—her voice shook—"why is Toto in there with you?"

"I am here enjoying being beautiful," said the Golden Boy. "And the little dog is here because I permitted him to slip through an opening in the wall. I can do that, you know—let small things enter or leave." He lifted a golden mirror and admired himself in it.

"But can't you leave?" asked Dorothy.

"Well, no," said the Golden Boy.

"Have you always been this way?" Dorothy asked.

"For a long, long time," came the grating, echoing answer. "Once I wasn't made of gold. Then one day a witch passed through the cornfield. She said she could make of me a thing of beauty. I have been so ever since."

"Do you like living like this?" asked Dorothy. "Why, you're a prisoner! You might as well be in . . . in . . . in the pokey—that's what we call jails in Kansas."

"Like it? Not like it?" said the Golden Boy. "It doesn't matter." He yawned and lifted the golden mirror, turning his head from side to side. "The profile is rather nice, don't you think? You must admire me very much."

"I'm not sure I do," said Dorothy. "The outside of you is beautiful, sure enough. But you seem to be—" What was there about the Golden Boy that was somehow all wrong? Dorothy's forehead puckered as she thought. "You seem to be very unfeeling," she finally said.

"When I turned into gold," said the Golden Boy, "my heart turned to gold too. It's hard. I feel nothing. But if we could see it, I'm sure we would agree that it is beautiful," he added proudly.

"Poor lad," murmured the Tin Woodman. "Oh, the poor lad."

The Golden Boy didn't seem to hear. He went on. "The witch told me I was the ugliest creature she had ever seen. She said it was a good thing I stayed in my cornfield so that nobody would have to look at me. It hurt me to hear that. It hurt like being stuck full of cockleburs. So she turned me into gold and I became beautiful. My heart became hard and unfeeling, true, but nothing ever again could hurt me."

"Are you happy now?" asked Dorothy.

"Happy?" The Golden Boy spoke slowly. "I

suppose I'm not. I feel nothing. I'm neither happy nor sad."

Toto yipped.

"Won't you let Toto go," pleaded Dorothy. "Why do you want to keep him? He can't make you happy."

"He amuses me, I think," said the Golden Boy. "I must say, it does get tiresome sitting here all the time, listening to the cornstalks grumble."

"You are mean and horrible and cruel," said Dorothy. "Just listen to Toto. He sounds so sad."

"But really," said the Golden Boy, "it's quite amusing, the way he keeps jumping against the wall and falling down, trying to get to you."

He laughed. His laughter sounded like icicles, made weak by a pale winter sun, falling and shattering.

Dorothy shivered.

Jinkeree, Junkeree, Joo

Dorothy turned to the others. "Whatever can we do?" she said. "I need Toto. I love you all, and I love Aunt Em and Uncle Henry. But all of you are with me only some of the time. Toto is with me all of the time, here or in Kansas. And, oh, I love him most of all."

"Be brave, Dorothy," said the Lion.

"Take heart, Dorothy," said the Tin Woodman.

"Think hard, Dorothy," said the Scarecrow. "I'll use my excellent brains to think hard too."

"Listen to me, all of you," said a sleepy voice. The sound, soft as dandelion fluff, drifted to Dorothy on the wind.

She spun around. Nobody was there.

"Here," said the gentle voice. "Over"—the speaker yawned—"here."

The voice came from some distance away, perhaps from among several pumpkins. Dorothy tiptoed toward them.

Lying in the shade of the biggest pumpkin was a caterpillar. It was a dainty yellow circled with bands of palest green. Its feelers were the color of the first rosy pink of dawn. It looked up at Dorothy, blinked sleepily, and yawned enormously.

"I have been waiting for someone to come," said the Caterpillar. "I think I have been waiting for you. But I could not have waited much longer, for it is long past time for me to go to sleep. I'm . . . not sure . . . I can stay awake long enough . . . to . . . tell . . . you . . . " Her eyes closed.

"Wake up!" Dorothy dropped to her knees. "Oh, do stay awake. What is it you must tell us?"

The Caterpillar's eyes opened. She yawned again. "I was here when the witch cast her spell," she said sleepily. "She told the boy that he was ugly. It wasn't true, but he believed her." Her eyes closed.

"Oh, please stay awake," pleaded Dorothy.

The Caterpillar's eyes opened. "So she turned him into a golden trinket that she could come here to admire. Now he's a prisoner and he feels nothing. He doesn't even know that he isn't happy." She blinked sleepily.

Around them the cornstalks rustled and moaned.

"She's going to sleep again," said Dorothy. "What can we do?"

Behind her, the Lion gave out a thunderous roar.

The Caterpillar's eyes popped open. "Mercy me!" she said in alarm.

"The Lion won't hurt you," said Dorothy. "He's only trying to help you stay awake."

"Thank you," breathed the Caterpillar.

"What did the witch say?" begged Dorothy. "Tell me before you fall asleep again."

"When she cast her spell," said the Caterpillar, speaking oh so slowly, "she said these words: 'Jinkeree, junkeree, joo. Gilly-gahatchee, gilly-gahoo.' And she said as she walked away that a

seven-leaf clover is very lucky. She said a wish upon one would break the spell, but that the boy would never find that out. And she cackled in an awful way." The Caterpillar shuddered, remembering.

Her eyes closed and opened. "Find such a clover," she said softly, yawning. "Ask the Golden Boy to wish upon it and say the words. I . . . hope you . . . find . . . "

She didn't finish. Her eyes remained closed. They didn't open even when the Lion gave another tremendous roar. Slowly the Caterpillar curled up, and as Dorothy watched, silken threads began to enclose her body.

"She's asleep," whispered the Lion.

"She's going to be a most beautiful butterfly," whispered the Scarecrow.

"All we have to do is find a seven-leaf clover," whispered the Tin Woodman, "and get the Golden Boy to wish on it, and he'll return to his old self. And then, of course, he'll let Toto go."

"All?" whispered Dorothy. "All? Oh, my! I've only found one lucky four-leaf clover in my whole life. Now I have to find one with seven leaves!"

5

The Weasel-Foxes

Dorothy led the way out of the enchanted cornfield. And now the twisted stalks opened a path away from the golden summerhouse. Behind her, growing fainter, were Toto's desperate barks and the hollow laughter of the Golden Boy.

At last they reached the edge of the cornfield. As the four friends stood looking around the countryside, the cornstalks gave a gusty sigh and then were silent.

"Before we can find a seven-leaf clover," said

Dorothy, "we must find a place where clover grows."

The area before them was marshland. Dorothy shaded her eyes with her hand. "There's a field of tall grass on the other side of the marsh," she said, pointing. "It stretches to a forest."

"Beyond those places there must be a meadow," said the Scarecrow, who always looked on the bright side of things. "We'll find clover there."

"But first we have to cross this marshland," said the Tin Woodman. "I'd really rather not get wet. Rust, you know."

Dorothy thought, studying the marsh. "There are spots of grass," she said. "Here's what we'll do. Getting wet won't hurt me, so I'll go first. I'll step on the dry places, and you walk in my footsteps."

She went first, testing, stepping from one grassy hummock to the next, choosing the driest.

Behind her walked the Tin Woodman, his arms outstretched to keep his balance. He put his feet carefully on the knobs of thick grass as Dorothy lifted her feet away from them.

The Scarecrow hopped after him. "Instead of

stepping stones," he said, "we have stepping *grass.*"

The Lion brought up the rear.

"We're getting there," Dorothy said encouragingly. "See? It's really quite easy. We just . . . have . . . to . . . " Her voice trailed away.

She tested one hummock, then another. Each time her foot sank into hidden water. She tried several more, then stood looking around. "There isn't another dry spot anywhere here," she said in a small voice.

The Lion edged past the others and came to her side. "I'm not awfully fond of water," he said, "but I can see what I must do. We aren't far from the tall grass. I'll carry each of you through this muddy place."

Dorothy climbed onto his back and held tightly to his thick mane. The Lion stepped forward. They sank at once until his legs were covered with mud and water. But then they sank no more.

Slowly, carefully, he slogged through the marsh and at last stepped onto dry earth.

"Oh," Dorothy said with a sigh, "thank you, dear Lion. A little water wouldn't hurt me, but I might have got stuck in the mud on the bottom."

The Lion shuddered. "I really don't like mud and such. Haven't since I was a cub. But friendship makes certain demands." He turned, went back through the marsh, and brought the Scarecrow and the Tin Woodman to safety.

The Tin Woodman looked down at his feet and found not a drop of water. He looked relieved.

"I turn into a ragbag of wet straw when I get wet," said the Scarecrow. "You'd have had to take out my straw and scatter it in the sun to dry before we could have gone on."

The Lion rolled in the tall grass until he was

free of water and mud. Fluffy and golden once more, he rose to his feet, ready to continue.

The grass stood well above Dorothy's head, so the Tin Woodman went first, keeping his eyes on the forest beyond.

They had been walking for some time when Dorothy heard a slithering sound. "Wait," she whispered.

They listened. Nothing.

"I must have imagined it," she said. But as soon as they began to move, the slithering sound returned.

The back of Dorothy's neck prickled. "Some-

one is following us," she said. "I can feel eyes watching us."

"Come out, cowards!" roared the Lion. "Show yourselves, like decent creatures."

The tall grass parted. Eyes peered out at them. Then, one by one, a band of weasel-foxes surrounded them. They had the short legs and long, low body of a weasel and the grinning, big-eared head of a fox. The cunning of both beasts, doubled, showed in their eyes.

The Scarecrow and the Tin Woodman crowded close to Dorothy to keep her safe.

"Stop where you stand!" thundered the Lion. "I

am King of the Beasts. Come no nearer."

The weasel-foxes snickered. "You are not our king," taunted their leader. "We give allegiance only to the Wicked Witch of the West."

"But she's dead!" said Dorothy, stepping from behind the Tin Woodman and the Scarecrow.

"Dead . . . dead . . . dead?" muttered the weasel-foxes.

"She melted away," said Dorothy, "when I threw a pail of water on her. How can you give allegiance to someone who's dead?"

"You killed her?" said the leader of the band. "Then we owe our allegiance to you."

Dorothy took a step backward. What a horrible idea!

"What is your command?" asked the leader.

"My command," Dorothy said firmly, "is that you take yourselves off to the farthest corner of Oz and stay there. You must never come out again."

"That'll be no fun," said the leader.

"No fun . . . no fun . . . no fun," muttered the others.

With that, the weasel-foxes slunk away. Their

snickers hung in the air long after they were gone.

"You did a wise thing, Dorothy," said the Scarecrow. "Oz will be a nicer place without them."

The friends pushed their way through the tall grass without further trouble. When they entered the cool shadows of the forest, the Lion took the lead. "My kind of wholesome animals live here," he said. "There will be no trouble from them."

And there was none. The friends hurried among the tall trees, with the birds twittering overhead, and came at last to the other side of the forest. Spread before them was a meadow. It reached to a distant blue river and almost as far as the eye could see on the left and right.

"Your meadow, Dorothy," said the Scarecrow, sweeping his arm around as though he were giving her a gift.

"But it's enormous," Dorothy said with a gasp. "How ever can I find a seven-leaf clover in this huge place! I'll have to hunt for days and days. And what will happen to poor little Toto while I'm gone?"

6

Clover!

"There are four of us," the Scarecrow said helpfully. "We can divide the meadow into four parts."

"That will speed things up," said the Tin Woodman.

"But it's still a huge place." Dorothy sighed.

"Now, see here." The voice came from behind them. "Who-oo"—the gentle voice rested on the word—"are all of you-oo?" Again the voice stroked the word. "I was feeling quiet and serene until you-oo came along. You have upset my mooood."

Lying in the shade of a big maple tree was a most dignified cow. She was the soft brown of late autumn leaves. Her horns were creamy in color and gracefully curved. The eyes that studied Dorothy and the others were large and brown, fringed with thick lashes.

"We beg your pardon, ma'am," said the Scarecrow, the very soul of politeness. "We didn't come here especially to upset you."

"We've come to help our little friend," said the Tin Woodman. "When we've found what we're looking for, we'll leave you to your mood."

"Indeed?" said the Cow. She lifted herself to her feet with great dignity and stepped slowly toward them. "When anyone is upset, I am upset too-oo. Though you-oo may not mean to-oo, you are up-setting my mooood. Would you care to-oo share with me what all this hullabaloo-oo is about?"

So Dorothy told the gentle animal about Toto and the Golden Boy and the field of twisted corn-stalks.

"A most entertaining story," said the Cow. "I do-oo so enjoy a good story."

"But it's hard to find even a four-leaf clover," said Dorothy. "I've never heard of one with seven leaves. And this is a great-huge meadow."

"Poor child," said the Cow. "You have lived a starved life, that is clear. In my time, I have seen them all—four-leaf, five, six, seven. Once I even found an eight-leaf clover. Of course, that was rare." A glazed look clouded her eyes as she re-membered. "It was delicious."

"You have?" said Dorothy. "I mean, seen them all?" Her spirits lifted. "Do you know, then, where I can find a seven-leaf clover?"

The Cow sniffed. "Do I know! My dear, I have been munching at this meadow since I was a calf. I know every inch of it. I know the tastiest greens, and I know those that are bitter. I know those that—"

"But the seven-leaf type," the Lion said impatiently. "That's what we have come for."

"Fuss, fuss, fuss," said the Cow. "I shall be pleased to help you-oo. But do not hurry me. There is much you must see here first."

And she set off, stepping in a most dignified manner, to show them around her meadow.

She stopped near some three-leaf clovers. "Crisp," she said. "Rather tangy. They work well in a salad. To be eaten *after* the main course, you know."

Next she led them to patches of four-leaf and five-leaf clover. Four-leaf clovers were "flat tasting." They "perked up" if eaten with "a pinch of mint." Five-leaf clovers were, she said, "more chewy, you know."

Next she paused near a clump of purple clover blossoms. "A nice little dessert," she said. "A bit sweet for my taste, but a pleasing ending to a light meal."

"I've tasted clover," said Dorothy. "Once I wanted to see why the bees like it. I pulled out each little tube of a flower and tasted the end. It was sweet."

"Mm-mm." The Cow didn't seem to hear. She had already turned to the next thing she wanted them to see, a patch of white clover blossoms. "Excellent," she said. "A milder dessert than the purple—"

The Lion had been grumbling softly, deep in his throat. "But the seven-leaf type, madame," he pleaded. "A seven-leaf clover is all that we need."

The Cow turned her great brown eyes on him. She stood tall and proud. "Tut, sir!" she said. "How can you-oo know what living is all about if you-oo rush around as you seem to do-oo. Do not, sir, try to force your willy-nilly way of life upon me, sir."

The Lion's grumbling ended. He padded meekly along with the others, learning more about meadows than any lion usually cares to know.

And so they heard about minced mushrooms. And herbs. "Oh, the wild herbs! Rosemary and sweet basil. Best eaten fresh, you know." Wild onions, declared the Cow, were "a taste treat worthy of—" She looked at the Lion. "Worthy of an emperor," she finished.

"Six-leaf clovers," she said, continuing the tour of the meadow, "are best dressed with dew, with a sprig of parsley on the side.

"But the seven-leaf clover," she said at last. She led them to a spot not far from the place where they had entered the meadow.

"After all this walking," grumbled the Lion— very, very softly.

"The seven-leaf clovers, my dears, are best eaten naturally, nothing added. A truly great and simple dish." She closed her eyes and lifted her nose into the air. "A delight to the tongue," she said softly.

At last! Dorothy dropped to her knees, counting the leaves. "They really do have seven! And there are lots and lots of them here. Heaps!"

"Pick a whole bunch," the Tin Woodman said grandly, "a regular bouquet. In case we lose some."

"Tut-tut, mustn't be greedy," said the Cow. "Two-oo will do-oo. And if one is left over, I shall be happy to take care of it for you-oo."

Dorothy rose, tucking two of the seven-leaf clovers into her pocket. "We can go back now," she said joyfully. "Now we can rescue Toto."

7

The Golden Boy

They went back the way they had come, through the forest, through the tall grass where now there were no weasel-foxes to bother them.

The Cow had joined them, for as she said, "I love a good story. But you couldn't tell me the end. I shall have to see that for myself."

"Welcome," the Lion had said. "But mind you, we move along faster than seems to be your custom."

And so the Cow followed at the pace Dorothy set—which was a steady jog.

Dorothy stopped at the edge of the marsh. What would they do now? The Lion would willingly carry them back across the muddy spots. But could he carry the Cow, too?

The Cow, panting, came to stand beside her. "And this is the marshland you-oo spoke of?"

Dorothy nodded. "The Lion carried us across."

"Indeed!" sniffed the Cow. "I'm sure you-oo were all too-oo busy racing about to hunt for the path through this bog."

"A path, madame?" asked the Lion.

"A sheep once mentioned that a path is here," said the Cow. "Bay leaves border it, she said. Bay leaves are, as you-oo may know, excellent for—"

"The path, madame," said the Lion, groaning. "The path!"

"If you knew flora as I know flora," said the Cow, "you could take yourself more safely around this world of ours."

But she left off her lecture on bay leaves and walked calmly along the edge of the marsh, stopping at several places for a taste of this or that.

She did in time find the bay leaves she sought, nibbled on one, said, "This way, if you please," and led them across a dry bridge of land that cut through the swamp.

On the far side, Dorothy returned to her swift jog. And so they came to the field of twisted cornstalks. Amid a chorus of sighs, it opened a path before them. But now Dorothy paid no attention to the way the cornstalks wove solidly behind them. She thought only of Toto.

"He isn't barking," she said softly, fearful of what that might mean.

"Keep your heart strong," said the Tin Woodman. "It will reach out to Toto."

As before, the cornstalks grew most thickly at the outer edge of the field. They thinned near the center, and so at last the friends burst into the clearing. There was the golden summerhouse, shimmering in the sunlight. Toto lay in the shadows inside, whimpering.

"Toto!" shouted Dorothy. "I've come back!"

The little dog jumped up and leaped at the golden wall, yipping happily.

Dorothy knelt as close as she dared. "It's all right, Toto," she said comfortingly. "I'm here now.

And I have a lucky seven-leaf clover for the Golden Boy to wish upon. Soon you'll be free."

"Do you really have a lucky clover?" came the hollow voice from inside the summerhouse. "And what does that have to do with me? But I must say I'm glad you've come back. The little dog doesn't amuse me much after all. When you went away he just lay there and whined."

Dorothy took one of the seven-leaf clovers from her pocket. She held it out on the palm of her hand. "You are under a terrible enchantment," she said. "But you can break the spell. You've only to wish on this lucky clover and say the magic words and you'll be your real self. You can feel happy about things again."

"That might be nice," said the Golden Boy. "But. . ." He paused for a long moment. "Everyone will laugh at me again, because I'll be ugly."

"Once I had no heart and felt nothing," said the Tin Woodman. "But even if things hurt sometimes, it's better to feel something than nothing."

Dorothy thought hard. She had to make the Golden Boy want to wish on the seven-leaf clover.

"You said that Toto didn't amuse you after we went away," she said. "So, if you don't make a wish—" She gulped. Could she really say it? "If you don't make the wish, *we'll* go away. You can just sit here and be bored forever. So there!"

She held her breath. Oh, she just could *not* go away and leave Toto forever. . . .

After a long moment the Golden Boy spoke. "Oh, all right. Since you are all so set against me, I will make the wish."

Dorothy tossed the seven-leaf clover toward an opening in the golden wall. A wind caught it and carried it inside, fluttering as a butterfly might.

The Golden Boy lifted his mirror and looked at himself a last time. "Pity," he murmured. "Such a pity." Then he picked up the seven-leaf clover.

"Say these words," said Dorothy, saying the witch's spell, "and make your wish."

"Jinkeree, junkeree, joo. Gilly-gahatchee, gilly-gahoo," said the Golden Boy. "I wish to become my old self again."

There was a gust of windy sighs, and the golden summerhouse untwisted itself. In its place stood a cluster of cornstalks at the peak of summer greenness. And all the cornstalks in the field around untwisted and stood tall, reaching for the blue sky as cornstalks should.

Toto ran from the clump of cornstalks, barking happily. Dorothy scooped him up and hugged him. She had never been so happy about anything in her whole life. Toto licked her chin.

But where was the Golden Boy? Dorothy looked around. "Where are you?" she called.

"Here," said a voice from the cluster of cornstalks where the golden summerhouse had stood. The voice that spoke was warm. "I'm here, all right. And I feel . . . I feel . . ." The voice sounded surprised and shy. "Why, I feel happy! What a wonderful feeling!"

"Oh, come out," said Dorothy. "Come out, please."

"You'll laugh," came the reply.

"But we won't," said Dorothy.

"Would someone who looks like me laugh at someone who looks like . . . whatever you look like?" asked the Scarecrow.

"Would a man of tin, with patches all over his tin skin, laugh at anyone?" asked the Tin Woodman.

"Promise?" came the shy question.

"I promise," said Dorothy. "May I turn into a sour dill pickle if I break my promise—that's what we say in Kansas, where I come from."

With that, the cornstalks parted and out stepped a boy. A Popcorn Boy.

8

A Great Popping and Snapping

The Popcorn Boy peered out at Dorothy from under the brim of his straw hat. "You're not laughing," he said timidly.

"And I won't, either, you can be sure of that," said Dorothy. "I've never seen a Popcorn Boy before," she added, studying him from the top of his hat to his toes, "and so I can't compare you with anyone else, but really, you're quite nice looking. You have a friendly face."

"That's comforting," said the Popcorn Boy.

"But then, you aren't like the others who poked fun at me."

"Well, they certainly weren't nice people," said Dorothy.

"Oh, they weren't *people*," said the Popcorn Boy. "Except for the witch, that is."

"If I may say so, I don't think you ought to count *her* as people either," said the Scarecrow.

"After the witch told me she could make me beautiful, she went away to fetch her magic potion," said the Popcorn Boy. "That very day, a pack of wolves passed through the cornfield. They ran in circles around me, howling. Their howls sounded like laughter. They howled long into the night. Even the moon seemed to smile."

"Wolves . . ." said Dorothy, remembering. Wolves had attacked her and the Lion and the Scarecrow and the Tin Woodman on their way to the castle of the Wicked Witch of the West.

"The very next morning," the Popcorn Boy went on, "a flock of wild crows swooped down into the cornfield. They flapped around me, screaming and laughing." A shadow of pain crossed his face. "They flew away crying 'Ugly, ugly, ugly!' "

"Crows are cruel," said the Tin Woodman. "I well remember how they attacked us in the country of the Wicked Witch of the West."

"If just one creature thought me ugly, maybe I would have turned it aside," said the Popcorn Boy. "But the wolves and the wild crows said exactly what the witch had said. I believed them."

"I think I'm beginning to see," said Dorothy.

"After that," said the Popcorn Boy, "there came a great cloud of black bees—"

"I knew it!" exclaimed Dorothy. "The witch was the Wicked Witch of the West. The wolves and crows and bees were the same ones she sent to attack us in the country she once ruled."

"She came back the next day with a magic potion," said the Popcorn Boy. "She sprinkled me with it, and I turned to gold. After that, when she came to admire me, she always told me I was handsome. But she always laughed when she said it. Sometimes I wondered why."

"She laughed because she had tricked you," said Dorothy. "She was pure mean—as mean as a snake caught in a hay fork. Being mean was *fun* for her."

"But you don't have to worry about her ever again," said the Lion. "She's dead. Dorothy threw a bucket of water on her and she just melted away."

"The wolves and the wild crows and the bees are dead too," said the Tin Woodman. "I know, for the Scarecrow and I killed them."

"That all happened long, long ago," said Dorothy. "Why, the witch turned you to gold even before I ever came to Oz the very first time. And you've been sitting here ever since, locked up and alone."

"Not alone," said a sweetly trilling voice.

Who had spoken? Dorothy looked around.

Stepping out of the silken cocoon that had enclosed the caterpillar was, not a butterfly, but a smiling girl. Her flowing hair was the pale, soft yellow of cornsilk. Her eyes were the green of the first new leaves of spring. And she was clothed in a fluttering gown of green that exactly matched the towering cornstalks.

"I was here," she said. "I saw the witch work

her magic on you and I promised myself to wait with you for someone to come to release you from her spell."

"But why didn't you speak to me?" asked the Popcorn Boy.

"I called to you while you were your own self," said the Cornsilk Girl. "You were so unhappy that you didn't hear me. After you became golden and beautiful, you thought of nothing but your mirror and your beauty. My words, the words of the caterpillar I was then, wouldn't have mattered to you."

The Popcorn Boy bowed his head. He stared in misery at the ground around his feet.

"But now . . . may I say . . . " the Cornsilk Girl said shyly, "you—I mean the real you—are far more beautiful than the Golden Boy."

The Popcorn Boy blushed. His shyness matched the Cornsilk Girl's, and for a moment he could not utter a word. "I have never seen anyone as pretty as you," he finally said.

The Cow sighed contentedly. "Oh, I do-oo love happy endings," she said. "It was worth the run just to see how things turned out."

Suddenly there was a shuffling among the tall, straight cornstalks that surrounded them, and a pleased hum filled the air.

"The twisted cornstalks are happy to be untwisted at last," said Dorothy.

With that, the cornstalks broke into a great popping and snapping. Popcorn filled the air, flying every which way. Great puffs of it danced and bounced on the green leaves before dropping to the earth. It began to pile up on the ground.

Ping, pong, pung—it bounced off the Tin Woodman's shiny body.

"Oo-oo-oo-oo," chuckled the Scarecrow, and he caught some of it in his hat.

"It smells all buttery and good!" Dorothy said with a laugh.

"Excuse me, my dear," whispered the Cow. "But may I trouble you for the extra seven-leaf clover? It wouldn't do-oo to waste it, you-oo know."

Dorothy dug it from her pocket and gave it to her. The Cow popped it into her mouth. She swallowed. Her eyes glazed over and she kissed the air. "Delectible . . . delicious," she murmured.

"I feel like a cub again," said the Lion. He lay on his back, like an enormous kitten, and batted at the popcorn with his paws. He sent showers of the feathery light stuff flying up into the air.

Toto barked. Dorothy hugged him and said, "There's nothing to be afraid of," and, "Oh, it tickles!" as the popcorn brushed against her nose. "Ah-hh—" She started to sneeze, reached for her handkerchief to smother the sneeze, and when she did—

"Choo!" She found herself back in Kansas, sitting in the grass under the apple tree, her pockets full of popcorn.

"I wasn't ready to come back to Kansas just yet," she wailed. "I didn't even get to the Emerald City to see Princess Ozma."

She tucked her handkerchief back into her pocket. "I must remember not to wave this without thinking when I'm in the Land of Oz. Princess Ozma saw me in her magic picture and thought I wanted to come back to Kansas."

Toto bounded from her lap, yipping, and chased a butterfly. Then he came back and settled down beside her, his tail waving like a small flag.

"Darling Toto," said Dorothy, "you are the only one who has been in the Land of Oz with me and here in Kansas as well. I'm so glad you weren't caught forever in the Golden Boy's summerhouse. But you must remember," she went on, "when we go to visit the Scarecrow and the Tin Woodman and the Cowardly Lion, that things in Oz aren't always what they seem to be."